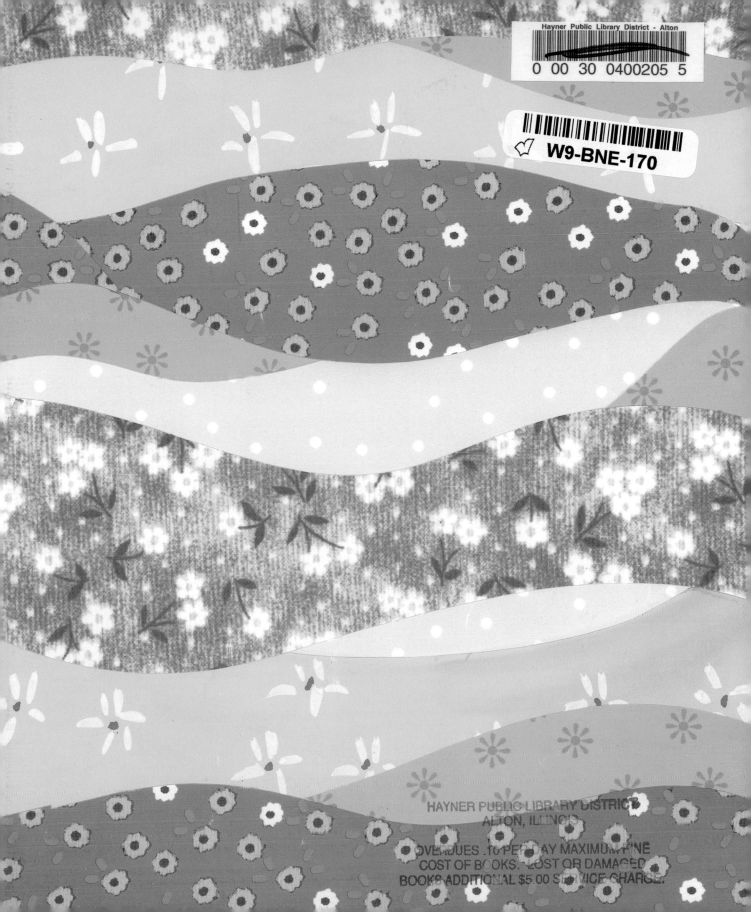

To my mom—and all the great moms around the world

Margaret K. McElderry Books ~ An imprint of Simon & Schuster Children's Publishing Division ~ 1230 Avenue of the Americas, New York, New York 10020 ~ Copyright © 2006 by Karen Katz ~ All rights reserved, including the right of reproduction in whole or in part in any form. ~ Book design by Lee Wade and Jessica Sonkin ~ The text for this book is set in Bembo. ~ The illustrations for this book are rendered in collage, gouache, and colored pencils. ~ Manufactured in China ~ 10 9 8 7 6 5 4 3 2 1 ~ Library of Congress Cataloging-in-Publication Data Katz, Karen. ~ Mommy hugs / by Karen Katz.—1st ed. ~ p. cm. ~ Summary: A loving mother counts the hugs she gives her baby throughout the day. ~ ISBN-13: 978-0-689-87772-8 ~ ISBN-10: 0-689-87772-2 (hardcover) ~ [1. Hugging—Fiction. 2. Mother and child—Fiction.] ~ I. Title: Mommy hugs. II. Title. ~ PZ7.K15745Mo 2006 [E]—dc22 ~ 2004025618

FIRST
EDITION

mommy hugs

by karen katz

MARGARET K. MCELDERRY BOOKS
NEW YORK LONDON TORONTO SYDNEY

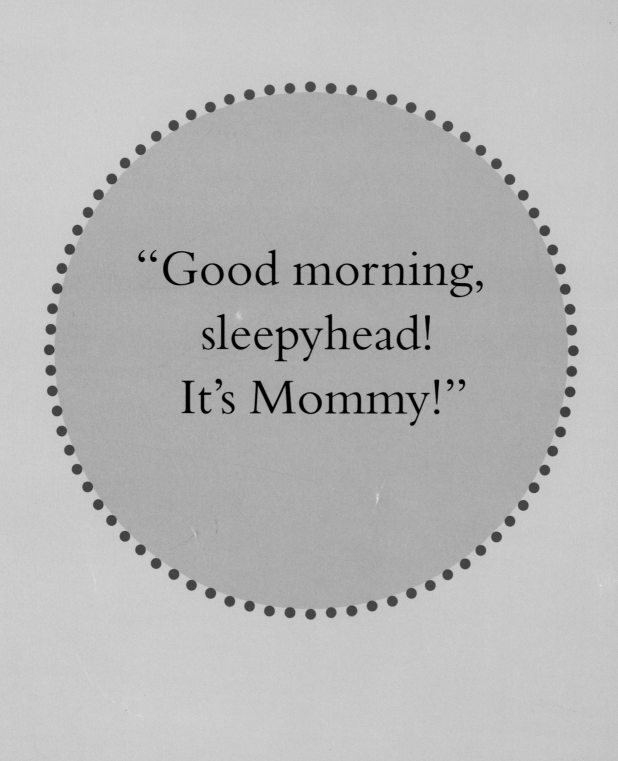

"Good morning,
sleepyhead!
It's Mommy!"

one nuzzle-wuzzle

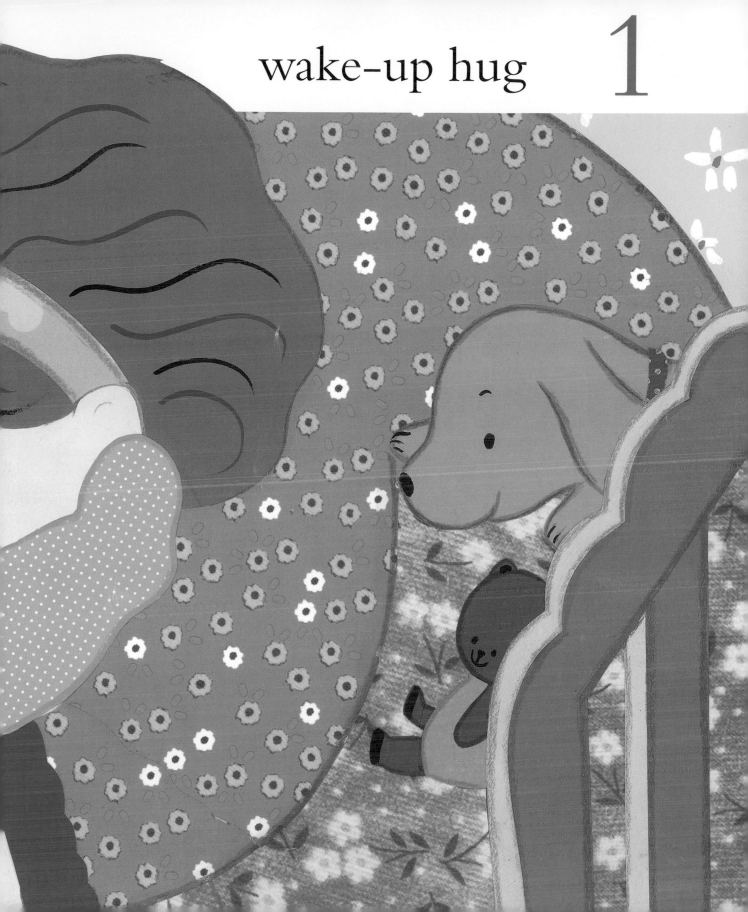

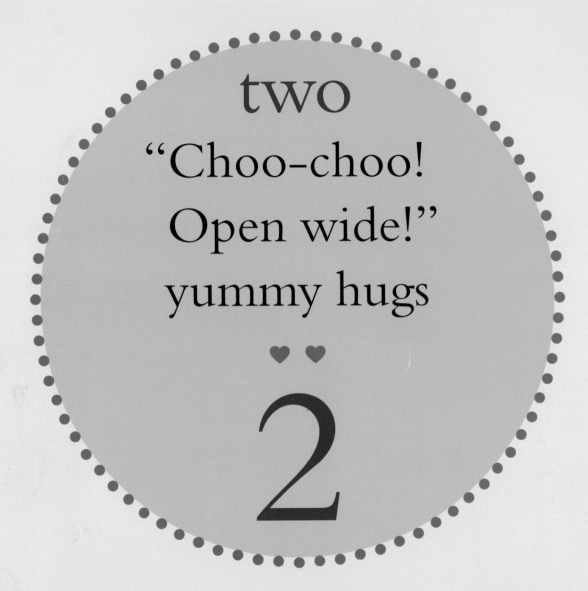

two
"Choo-choo!
Open wide!"
yummy hugs

♥ ♥

2

three

"We're off to the park" piggyback hugs

♥ ♥ ♥

3

♥ ♥ ♥ ♥ ♥ four "I'll always catch

you!" sliding hugs

five
"Mommy will fix it!"
don't-cry hugs
♥ ♥ ♥ ♥ ♥
5

six "You said *Mama!*"

first-word hugs

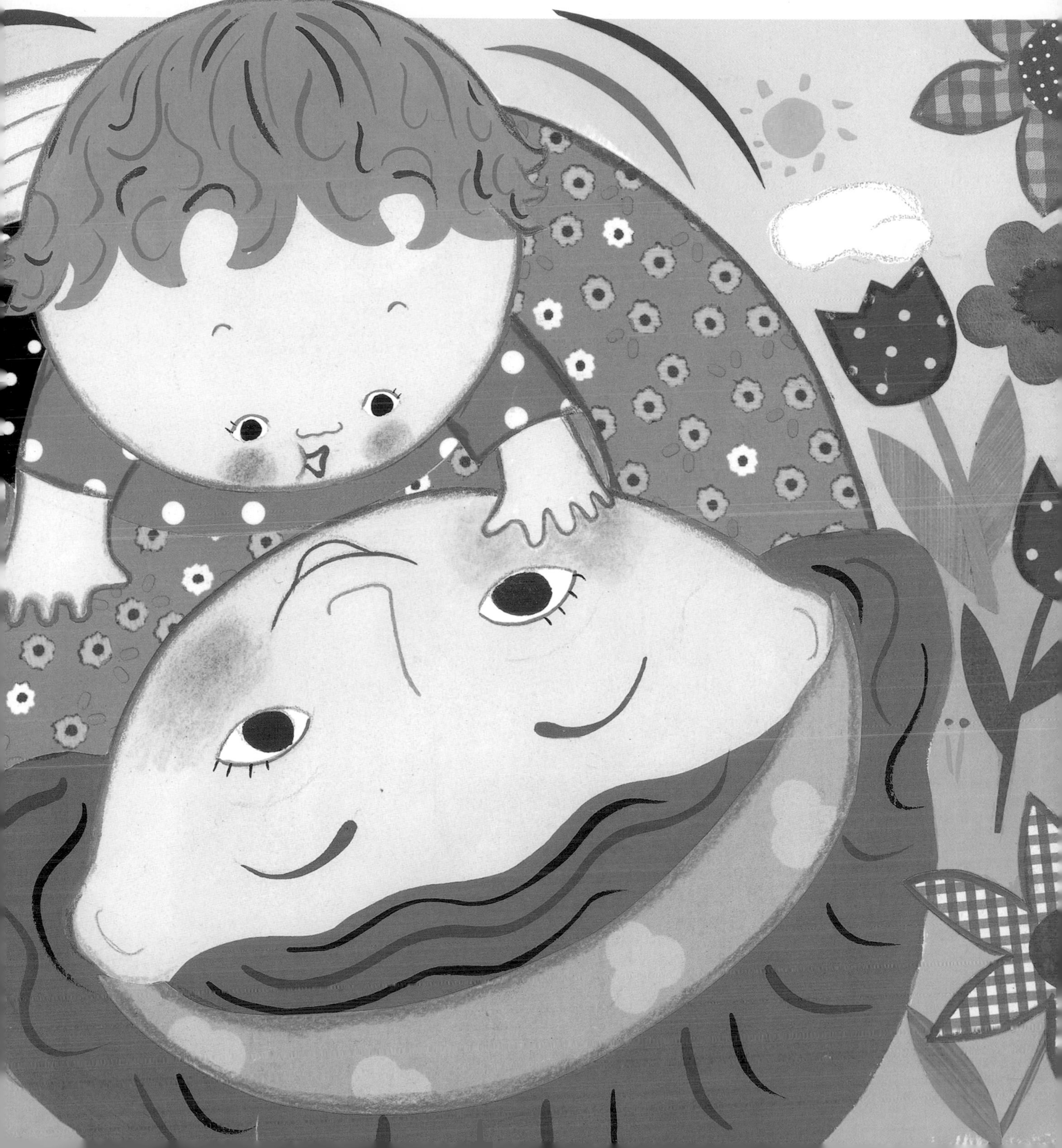

seven

splishy, splashy
bathtub hugs

♥ ♥ ♥ ♥ ♥ ♥ ♥

7

eight

"Who made this mess?" laughing hugs

♥ ♥ ♥ ♥ ♥ ♥ ♥ ♥ ♥

8

nine

"Who's a tired baby?"
night-night hugs

♥ ♥ ♥ ♥ ♥ ♥ ♥ ♥ ♥

9

ten

"I love you, I love you,
I love you, I love you,
I love you, I love you,
I love you, I love you,
I love you, I love you!"
good-night hugs

♥ ♥ ♥ ♥ ♥ ♥ ♥ ♥ ♥ ♥

10

Sleep tight,
little baby.

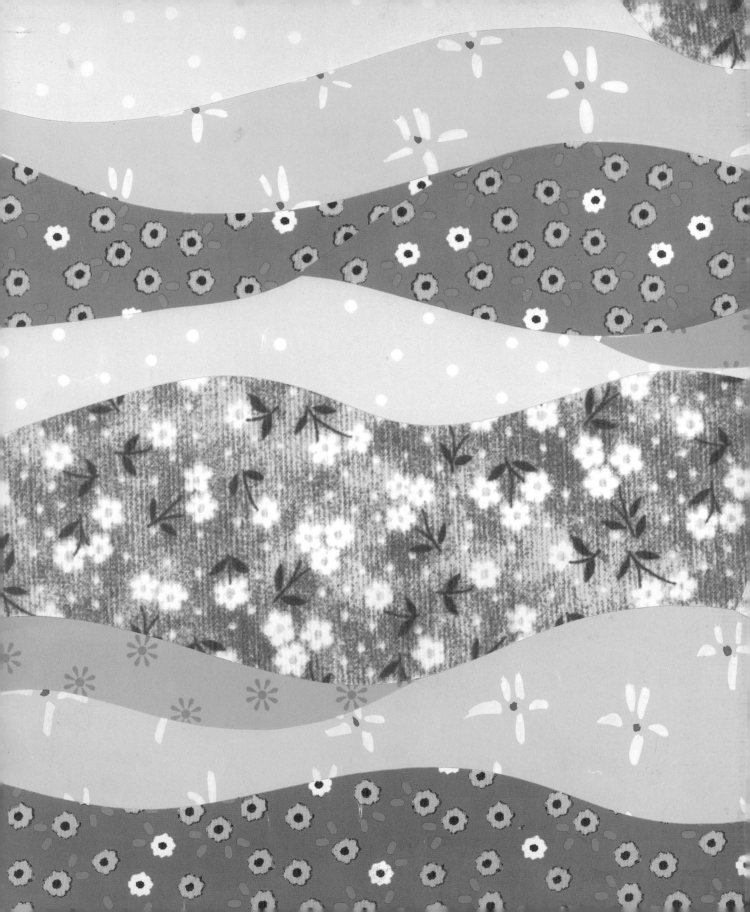